GEORGIE
and the Robbers

by ROBERT BRIGHT

SCHOLASTIC BOOK SERVICES
NEW YORK · TORONTO · LONDON · AUCKLAND · SYDNEY · TOKYO

Copyright © 1963 by Robert Bright. This edition is published by Scholastic Book Services, a
division of Scholastic Magazines, Inc., by arrangement with Doubleday & Co., Inc.

19 18 17 16 15 14 13 12 11   8 9/7 0/8

Printed in the U.S.A.

This is Georgie, the gentle little ghost. He lives in the Whittaker house. Every night, as everybody knows, Georgie has to creak the stairs and squeak the parlor door to remind Mr. and Mrs. Whittaker that it's time to go to bed and to sleep.

But Georgie never scared anybody. He was much too shy for that. So he had no idea of what he might have to do if strangers came into the house.

Now one night Mr. and Mrs. Whittaker went to a church sociable in the village. And just as usual, they didn't even bother to lock the door.

They never gave a thought to all the cozy antique furniture they had

— like the cozy old rocker on the porch where Miss Oliver the owl sometimes liked to perch

— or like the comfortable old sofa in the parlor where Herman the cat often snoozed

— or like all the
things that cluttered up
the attic where Georgie lived.

There wasn't an attic anywhere
that was more cluttered than
Georgie's attic. It was full
of old things no one could bear
to part with.

Now, old things like that are
antiques and worth a lot of
money. That is why there are
people who sometimes try to
steal them.

That night, after the Whittakers had
left the house, two strangers came
down the country road. They drove a
fast truck and wore masks.

They were robbers.

They took the rockers from the Whittaker's porch because they were old and antique.

And they took the sofa from the parlor
because it was even older than the
rocking chairs and more antique.

But from Georgie's attic they took everything — *every last thing* — because everything
up there was the oldest and most antique
of all.

Now that was a fine how-do-you-do!

Herman ran after the truck and Georgie ran after Herman.

But the robbers went so fast, they would have gotten clean away if it hadn't been for Miss Oliver. She flew high under the moon and watched them.

Suddenly she heard a bang. The robbers' truck had a blowout.

Miss Oliver flew after the robbers and saw
where they hid the truck to fix the tire.

It was in the barn, where the harmless cow lived.
The robbers drove the truck in and they put
the cow out of her own barn.

Miss Oliver flew straight back
to tell Herman and Georgie.

Herman decided that he had
better run to the village to
warn Mr. and Mrs. Whittaker
and the policeman.

But Georgie and Miss Oliver went
to be with the cow in the meadow.

When they got to the barn, they all knew there was just one
thing to do: *They must scare the robbers away.*

The cow couldn't scare the robbers, she was much too harmless. Miss Oliver couldn't scare the robbers, she was just a soft fuzzy owl. But Georgie was a ghost, and maybe he should have been able to scare *somebody*.

But Georgie was such a gentle ghost —

he

was

so

little...

"Oh, if I could only be a big scary ghost, just for once,"
Georgie thought.

Just then a wind came and began to billow the cover that kept the hay dry on the haystack in back of the barn.

And Georgie looked at the cow and he looked at Miss Oliver and he looked at the haystack. And although he was a very small ghost, Georgie had a really BIG IDEA.

Now the robbers were inside the barn fixing the tire, and they were already quite nervous.

Suddenly something came to the window, and it said mooooo...

And that bothered the robbers although they knew it must be a cow.

Next, something flew
under the eaves, and
it said whooooo...

And that startled the
robbers although they
knew it must be
an owl.

But then something else flitted past the door, and it said boooooo...

And that made the robbers both jump and drop their tools.

Because they knew that a cow said mooooo...And they knew that an owl said whooooo...But what was it that said BOOOOOOOOOOO?

The robbers were so upset they had to go outside and look.

Now what they saw at the corner of
the barn was the flick of a white tail.

But while it made their teeth chatter,
they weren't scared enough to run.

So they turned the corner of the barn and saw the flutter of white wings and one half of one big eye.

But while it made their knees knock together, they weren't scared enough to run.

So then they tip-toed to the next
corner of the barn...

And there
they saw the
biggest ghost
in the world.

That was enough to
scare anybody!

The robbers ran, and they ran...

They ran straight into the
arms of the village policeman.

But Georgie was so surprised
at himself for what he had
done, he ran too.

He ran and he ran...

He ran straight home to tell
the mice how he scared the robbers.

That same night the neighbors helped put the rocking chairs
back on the porch and the sofa back in the parlor again.

But best of all, they began putting everything
—*every last thing*—back into the attic again,
until it was properly cluttered with all
the nice old things no one could bear to
part with.

And Georgie would stand on the old trunk and show the mice what had happened at the cow barn. He showed them over and over...

And every night he creaked the stairs and squeaked the parlor door again.

But...although Georgie knows, and the mice know, and Herman knows, and Miss Oliver knows, and the cow knows, and although you and I know, not even until this very day do the Whittakers know who scared the robbers.